Community Helpers and **BUILDERS**

Building Places to
Play

Designed by
Amy Li

Written by
William Anthony

KidHaven
PUBLISHING

Published in 2023 by KidHaven Publishing,
an Imprint of Greenhaven Publishing, LLC
29 East 21st Street
New York, NY 10010

© 2021 Booklife Publishing
This edition is published by arrangement with
Booklife Publishing

Edited by:
Robin Twiddy

Designed by:
Amy Li

Cataloging-in-Publication Data

Names: Anthony, William, 1996-.
Title: Building places to play / William Anthony.
Description: New York : KidHaven Publishing,
2023. | Series: Community helpers and
builders | Includes glossary and index.
Identifiers: ISBN 9781534541054 (pbk.) |
ISBN 9781534541078 (library bound) |
ISBN 9781534541061 (6 pack) |
ISBN 9781534541085 (ebook)
Subjects: LCSH: Playgrounds--Juvenile
literature. | Community development--Juvenile
literature.
Classification: LCC GV423.A58 2023 |
DDC 711'.558--dc23

Manufactured in the United States of America

CPSIA compliance information: Batch #CSKH23: For further information contact
Greenhaven Publishing LLC, New York, New York at 1-844-317-7404.

Please visit our website, www.greenhavenpublishing.com.
For a free color catalog of all our high-quality books,
call toll free 1-844-317-7404 or fax 1-844-317-7405.

Find us on 🅕 🅘

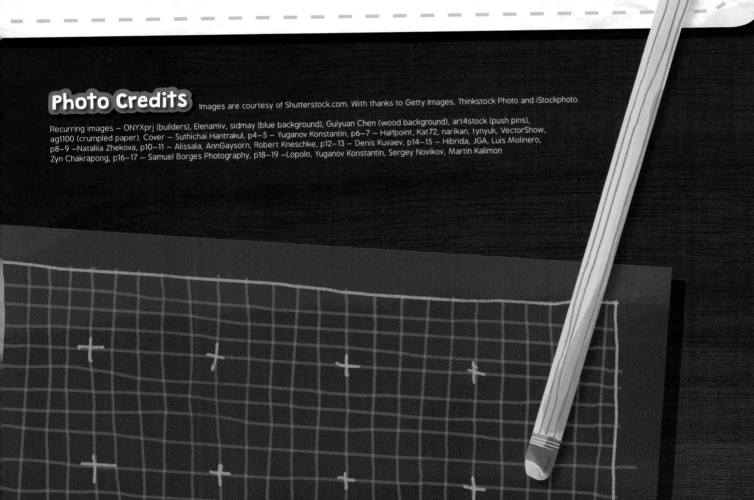

Photo Credits

Images are courtesy of Shutterstock.com. With thanks to Getty Images, Thinkstock Photo and iStockphoto.

Recurring images – ONYXprj (builders), Elenamiv, sidmay (blue background), Guiyuan Chen (wood background), art4stock (push pins),
ag1100 (crumpled paper). Cover – Suthichai Hantrakul, p4–5 – Yuganov Konstantin, p6–7 – Halfpoint, Kat72, narikan, tynyuk, VectorShow,
p8–9 –Nataliia Zhekova, p10–11 – Alissala, AnnGaysorn, Robert Kneschke, p12–13 – Denis Kuvaev, p14–15 – Hibrida, JGA, Luis Molinero,
Zyn Chakrapong, p16–17 – Samuel Borges Photography, p18–19 –Lopolo, Yuganov Konstantin, Sergey Novikov, Martin Kalimon

Contents

Page 4   Meet the Local Area Builders

Page 6   Park

Page 10   Kids' Club

Page 14   Playground

Page 18   Sports Club

Page 20   Our Local Area

Page 22   Your Local Area

Page 24   Glossary and Index

Words that look like <u>this</u> can be found in the glossary on page 24.

Meet the
Local Area Builders

Hi there! We're the Local Area Builders. We help <u>communities</u> by building the things they need in their local area. This area doesn't seem very fun, does it? There's not even anywhere to play!

Welcome to Playtown

New Place Needed:

Open-Air Antics

Playing outdoors is the best. It can be super sunny and there's lots of fresh air. I think we should build a place where all the kids can go and play outdoors!

— Grace, age 6

We need somewhere to play — let's get started!

Park

A park is the perfect place for kids to play! Parks are big, open areas with lots of space to run around and play games.

Tag is my favorite game to play at the park.

The park is a great place for me to take my dog for a walk.

Many parks have sports fields in them. Some parks have baseball or soccer fields. There's so much to do at the park!

7

Map Update

That park will give us kids lots of open space to play and have fun! Let's add a place for sports at the park too!

Park

Sports field

New Place Needed:

A Place for Pals to Play

I want a place to hang out with all my friends where there are a lot of fun things to do. Could we build a place like that, with games and other **activities**?

— Jake, age 5

Of course we can! Let's build!

Kids' Club

This club will be awesome. I can't wait to make new friends!

Kids' Club

A kids' club is a place where kids can go to play, meet friends, and do lots of fun stuff.

I can't wait to make different things at the kids' club to show my mom!

At a kids' club, you might spend your day making art or playing team games. You will usually be looked after by a group of adults.

Map Update

I can't wait to go to our new kids' club! I might make the Local Area Builders a cool badge while I'm there.

Kids' club

New Place Needed:

A Place for Play

I visited a different town and they had an awesome playground with lots of things to play on. Can we build one here too?

— Tara, age 5

That sounds like a great idea! Let's go!

Playground

A playground has lots of things to play on. It may have swings, a slide, and even a climbing frame.

Monkey bars are my favorite thing at the playground.

So we will have a playground at school and one near my house? I can't wait!

Playgrounds are a fun place to play games, such as <u>hopscotch</u>, and get some <u>exercise</u>.

Map Update

I can't believe it! There are so many places to play and there are more to come! This might be the best local area yet!

Playground

New Place Needed:

A Sporty Spot

My feet are always moving. Sometimes I run, jump, or just tap, tap, tap my toes. Could we make a place where I can use all my **energy**?

– Angelica, age 7

Another place to play? Let's do it!

Sports Club

I'm going to be a soccer player when I'm older. A sports club will help me practice!

A sports club will be a great place for kids to be energetic. A sports club may have a big gym and lots of <u>pitches</u> outside.

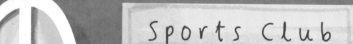

Sports Club

I'm going to learn how to play hockey. I can't wait!

Many sports clubs have team games to play, such as hockey, basketball, and volleyball. There are lots of chances to practice teamwork and get better at your favorite sport.

Our Local Area

That sports club completes our local area. This community now has many places for playing. It looks like a fun place to live!

Playground

Kids' club

Park

Sports field

Court

Sports club

Pitch

Your Local Area

It's time to try creating a local area yourself! Get a piece of paper and draw a map like the one on page 4.

What's going to be in your local area? Are there parks and playgrounds?

Theme park

Big bounce house

Think about your local area. Draw all the places where you can play on your map. Or you could make one up and go completely bonkers! It's up to you!

My house

Giant trampoline

What's in your made-up local area? What about a giant bouncy castle or a gigantic swimming pool?

Glossary

activities	things that are done for fun or for work
communities	groups of people who live and work in the same place
energy	the power to be active and do something
exercise	physical activity that is done in order to become stronger and healthier
hopscotch	a game in which players hop through a set of squares drawn on the ground
pitches	areas that are used for playing sports

Index

friends 9–10, 21
games 6, 9, 11, 15, 19
outdoors 5

sports 7–8, 17–20
teams 11, 19